Mama, Beth and me.

Just Beth and me.

Then we found Gary.

When We Married Gary

by Anna Grossnickle Hines

 Greenwillow Books, New York

It used to be just Mama, Beth, and me.

We played together and worked together.
Sometimes Mama got impatient and scolded.

Sometimes she got silly and danced with us in the kitchen.
We sat in three chairs at the table to eat our supper, and then Mama would read us stories and sing lullabies and tuck us in to sleep.

Beth said we had a daddy once, but he went away.
Mama said he had problems and wasn't ready for a family. She said it was too bad, and he didn't know what he was missing because we are her treasures.
Beth missed him and was sad sometimes, but I couldn't remember.

Then we got Gary.
When he came for supper, we sat in four chairs, and he helped Mama wash the dishes.
Beth and I saw them dancing in the kitchen . . . and we saw them kiss.

When we married Gary, Beth and I wore the wedding rings on ribbons around our necks, and we all held hands.

Gary said that since we already had
a daddy, we could call him Papa if we
wanted.
We made a card for him on Father's Day.

Gary's a forest ranger. Sometimes we go to work with him and walk around the campground to invite everyone to the campfire programs. Beth and I show the campfire lighters how to gather pine needles and twigs and get the fire ready to light.

But Gary can only pick us to be campfire lighters once each summer. He says it wouldn't be fair to treat us special, even though we are.

Beth is still a little sad about our daddy
sometimes, because she remembers. But
I think it's kind of like we're a puzzle—
Mama, Beth, and me. Our daddy didn't
fit with us, but Gary does.
Now we have four to work together
and play together and four at
the table for supper.

Sometimes Gary gets impatient with us,
just like Mama.

Sometimes he tells us stories, and sometimes he plays his guitar and sings. When he's feeling silly, he sings the *Wizard of Oz* song and clicks his heels together to make us laugh. He calls us his rascals . . .

and we call him Papa.

When we got married.

For Gary, because he fits with us, and for Sarah,
because she said it so well

Watercolor paints and colored pencils were used for the
full-color art. The text type is Novarese Medium.

Library of Congress Cataloging-in-Publication Data

Hines, Anna Grossnickle.
When we married Gary / by Anna Grossnickle Hines.
    p.   cm.
Summary: Beth still remembers the daddy who went
away, although her younger sibling does not, but both
of them accept Gary and call him Papa.
ISBN 0-688-14276-1.   [1. Stepfathers—Fiction.
2. Remarriage—Fiction.   3. Family life—Fiction.]
I. Title.   PZ7.H572Wj   1996   [E]—dc20
95-1627   CIP   AC